D1685339

This book belongs to:

91120000428313

For my mother and for Mauri

BRENT LIBRARIES

EAL

91120000428313

Askews & Holts	06-Mar-2020
JF	£6.99

This paperback edition first published
in 2020 by Andersen Press Ltd.
First published in Great Britain in 2019 by
Andersen Press Ltd., 20 Vauxhall Bridge Road,
London SW1V 2SA. Copyright © Eva Eland 2019.
The right of Eva Eland to be identified as the author
and illustrator of this work has been asserted by her in
accordance with the Copyright, Designs and Patents Act, 1988.
All rights reserved. Printed and bound in China.

10 9 8 7 6 5 4 3 2 1

British Library Cataloguing in Publication Data available.
ISBN 978 1 78344 795 4

The illustrations for this book were drawn by hand then risographed
before being printed in Pantone 486U, Pantone 3278U and Pantone 154U.

Eva Eland

WHEN
SADNESS
COMES TO CALL

Andersen Press

Sometimes Sadness
arrives unexpectedly.

It follows you around...

And sits so
close to you,
you can hardly
breathe.

You can try to hide it.

But it feels like you've become Sadness yourself.

Try not to be afraid
of Sadness.
Give it a name.

Listen to it. Ask where it comes
from and what it needs.

If you don't understand
each other, just sit together
and be quiet for a while.

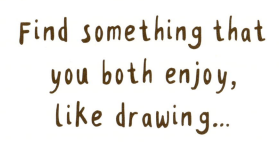

Find something that
you both enjoy,
like drawing...

listening to music...

or drinking hot
chocolate.

Maybe Sadness doesn't
like to stay inside.

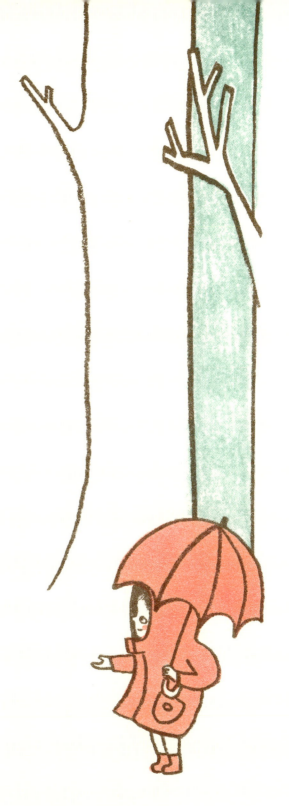

Try letting it out sometimes.

Go for a walk
through the trees.

You can listen to
their sounds together.

Maybe all it wants to know
is that it is welcome.

And to sleep, knowing
it is not alone.

When you wake up,
it might be gone.

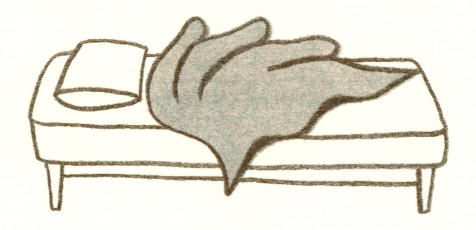

Don't worry - today is a new day.

Also by Eva Eland

WHERE HAPPINESS BEGINS